For Inga

Copyright © 2002 by Michael Neugebauer Verlag, an imprint of
Nord-Süd Verlag AG, Gossau Zürich, Switzerland
First published in Switzerland under the title Rudi Riese.
English translation © 2002 by North-South Books Inc., New York

First published in the United States, Great Britain, Canada,
Australia, and New Zealand in 2002 by North-South Books, an imprint
of Nord-Süd Verlag AG, Gossau Zürich, Switzerland.

Distributed in the United States by North-South Books Inc., New York.

Library of Congress Cataloging-in-Publication Data is available.
A CIP catalogue record for this book is available from The British
Library.

ISBN 0-7358-1620-4 (trade edition)   10 9 8 7 6 5 4 3 2 1
ISBN 0-7358-1621-2 (library edition) 10 9 8 7 6 5 4 3 2 1
Printed in Italy

For more information about our books, and the authors and artists
who create them, visit our web site: www.northsouth.com

Giant Jack

By Birte Müller
Translated by
J. Alison James

A Michael Neugebauer Book
North-South Books
New York / London

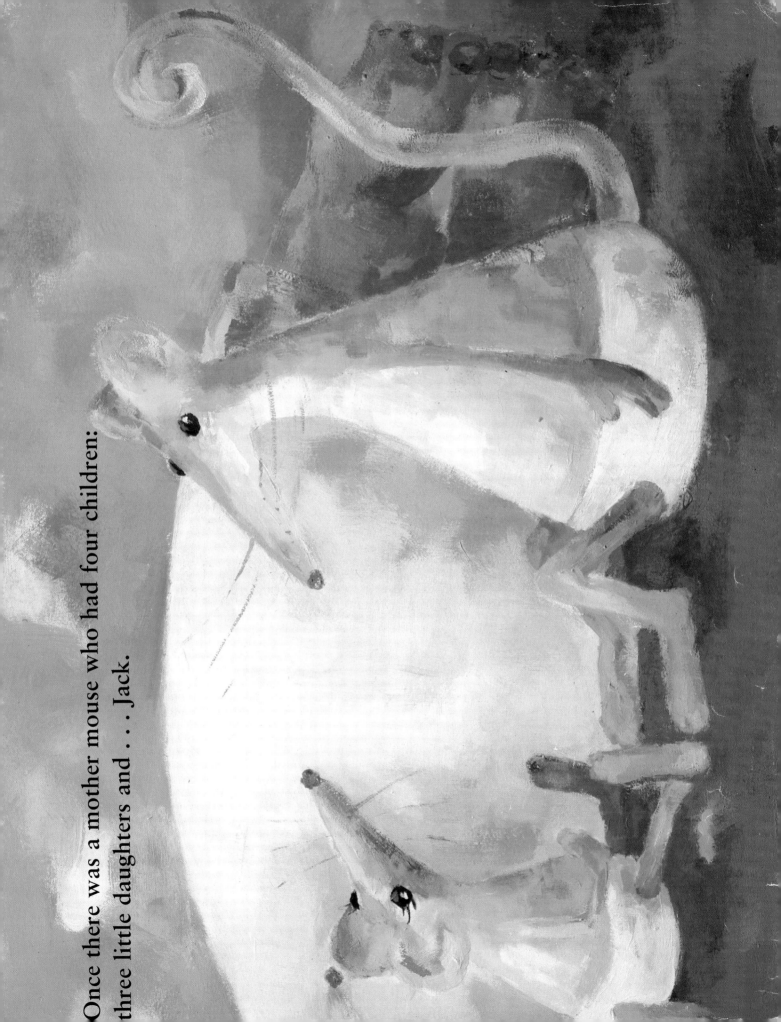

Once there was a mother mouse who had four children: three little daughters and . . . Jack.

From the beginning, Jack was much bigger than his sisters. "Jack is a giant," teased the mouse girls, and they giggled behind their paws.

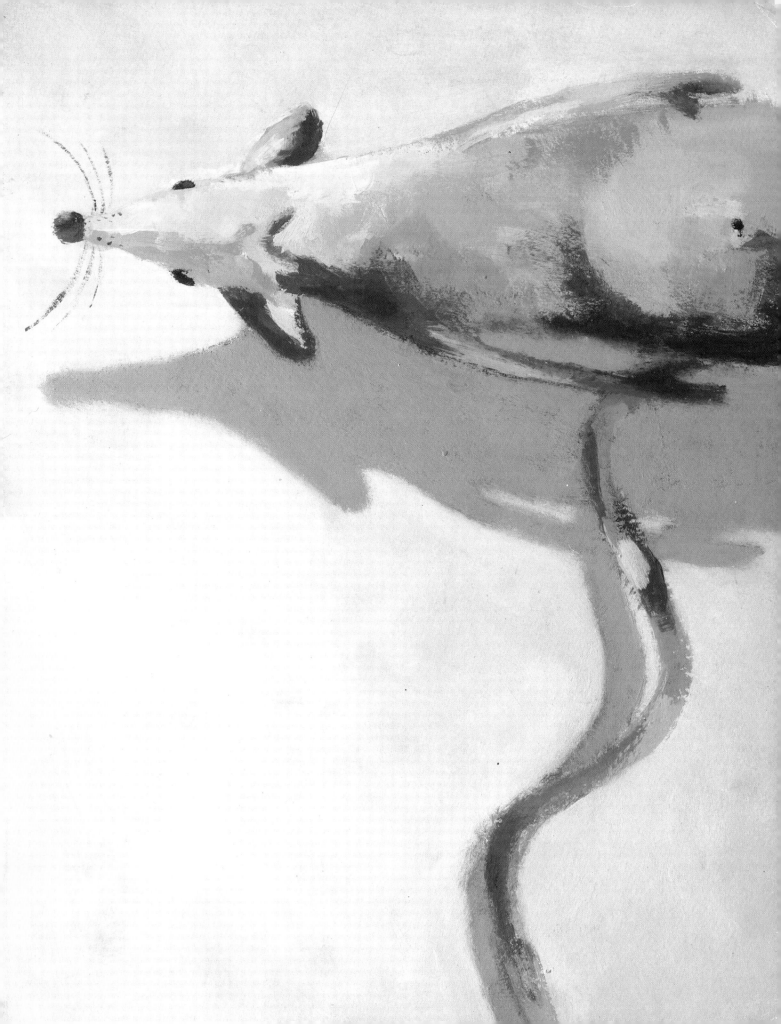

"Come on, Jack, dance with us!"
they would call
But Jack was clumsy, and his long tail
always got in the way

When the girls played hopscotch, Jack's feet were too big to fit in the spaces between the lines.

And one day, when he got stuck in the door to the mouse house, the three mouse girls laughed themselves silly. ...ack grew sadder and sadder.

"Why am I so big and ugly?" Jack asked his mother. "Why am I so different from my sisters?"

Mother Mouse stroked Jack's soft ears.

"You're not ugly at all, Jack," she said.

"And there is a good reason why you are different from the girls."

"I found you when you were a tiny baby. You were all alone. I loved you at once. I loved you so much that I brought you home with me. The truth is, Jack, you are not a mouse child. You are a rat child. You run like a rat and leap like a rat and swim like a rat. You're my big, strong son, and I love you."

"You look different because you came from a different family. But you belong to our family now—and you always will."

From then on, Jack was transformed. He didn't feel clumsy or ugly anymore. Quite the contrary. Jack discovered just how good he was at lots of things.

The three mouse girls now saw how great it was to have a big brother like Jack.
With him in the game, they won every time!

And he was always thinking up fun new games to play. "Jack is just rat-strong!" the girls bragged, and they were right.

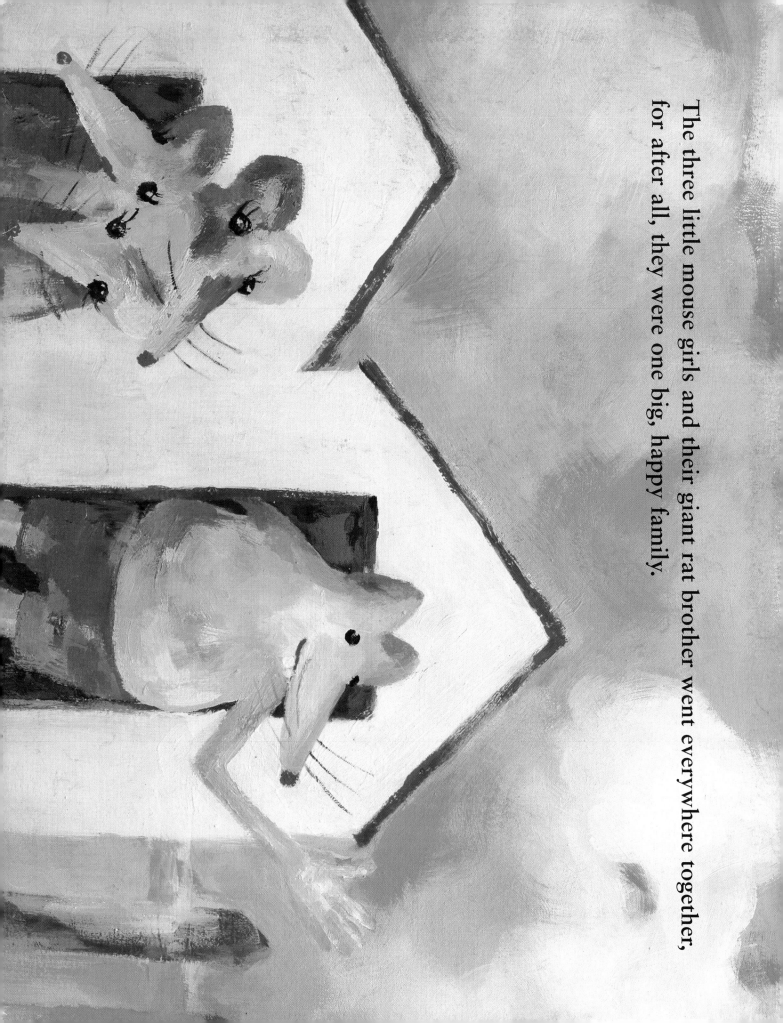

The three little mouse girls and their giant rat brother went everywhere together, for after all, they were one big, happy family.